TAKE YOU DOWN

FIRE & DESIRE BOOK 2

D. ROSE

PLAYLIST

hit different x sza & ty dolla sign
playing games x summer walker
thats why i love you x sir & sabrina claudio
streets x doja cat
in my head x ariana grande
touchdown x sir
otw x khalid, black & ty dolla sign
kiss it better x rihanna
you belong to me x trey songz
hungover x cassie
toronto x siah anlegra
can you handle it? x usher
mortal x baby rose
when we x tank
do you want to? x escape

take you down

nidhidrose.com

the playlist

PLAYLIST

spotify

PLAYLIST

apple music

TAKE YOU DOWN

CONTENTS

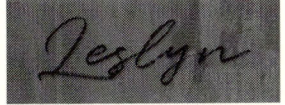

Do Not Answer: I miss you, Ifemi. Call
me back…

*W*hile rolling my eyes, I dropped my phone back into my clutch. I wanted to believe that Ogun missed me, but I knew it was all a game to him. That was cool, though. Because two could play that game. With a smile, I returned my attention to my date, Carson. He was going on and on about the current political climate, which was boring as hell. I fought the urge to yawn by reaching for my wine glass and bringing it to my lips. Not even a glass of Sauvignon Blanc could save me from this boredom.

It was our second date, and once again he led the conversation with a topic that I found uninteresting. Luckily, he was cute and had a voice as comforting as my big mama's apple pie with a scoop of vanilla ice cream on top. A smile graced his handsome features, making me smile.

Carson was *cool*.

He talked too much, and he had gotten too comfortable too soon. He wasted no time telling me every single detail about his life. He talked about growing up in Delaware, his siblings, and past relationships. He didn't miss a beat. I was kind of turned off by his willingness to tell me everything about him so soon.

The waiter stopped by to bring me another glass of wine and asked if we wanted to see the dessert menu. Before I could decline, Carson asked for the menu, adding at least another thirty minutes to our date. Nervously, I adjusted the rose gold Bulgari necklace Ogun had gifted me for Valentine's Day. Once I realized the chain was from him, my arm dropped to my lap.

"Cheesecake or apple pie?" Carson asked.

"Apple pie," I said with a weak smile.

He was genuinely enjoying himself and I was not.

"Earlier, you said you moved here from Jersey?"

I nodded. "Yup. My dad got a job working for the government, so we moved to Maryland when I was fifteen."

Carson scoffed and shook his head. "Starting high school in a new state? I couldn't imagine how that went."

"It went exactly how you thought it did." I sat back in my seat, feeling more relaxed.

Thinking about my first day of high school always lightened my mood. Back then, it felt like the end of the world, but now, I appreciated every trial and tribulation I experienced. Never had I been a shy girl. I made friends quickly and joined as many clubs and teams as I could. During my adolescent years, my parents were my least favorite people. I did whatever was necessary to keep busy. Now, they were my everything. Going away for college helped our relationship a lot.

"I bet you were a cheerleader in high school," Carson said with a sparkle in his eye.

The two glasses of wine I'd consumed were now coursing through my veins. My eyes lowered, and a smirk rested on my lips.

"Actually, I was." Bringing my wine to my lips, I took a sip. "And I was captain of the squad my senior year."

Carson smiled as his eyes did a quick sweep over me. "I'm not surprised."

I smiled, wondering if this would last past tonight. Probably not, though.

His conversation was a little dull, but I found him attractive. In just two dates, Carson had shown me different sides of him. La Vie, the restaurant he'd taken me to, differed from our first date at Top Golf. After telling him the last restaurants I'd been to, he brought me to a place similar to them. I didn't need fancy five-star dates to impress me, though. Those were just the perks that came with being attached to Ogun.

The feeling of my phone vibrating in my lap made my smile drop as I already knew who it was. Looking down, I opened my clutch and declined the call.

"You need to get that?" Carson asked with furrowed eyebrows.

Waving my hand, I replied, "No. It can wait."

He smiled, then reached for his drink. My phone vibrated again; this time, I didn't acknowledge it. Carson deserved my undivided attention. Since meeting him at the gym, he'd been persistently trying to get my number, and finally, I gave in. We talked on the phone for two weeks and had four workout dates before he asked to take me on an actual date.

Dating was still new to me. In college, meeting up for a happy hour or at the diner after a party was about all I did in terms of dating. Back then, every man I messed with knew I was there for a good time, not a long time. After leaving my strict parents behind for college, I was determined to enjoy myself. Watching my friends go through the same bullshit with different men turned me off from relationships. I wasn't interested in having someone clock my moves, the way I dressed, or how many parties I went to in a month. I wanted complete and total freedom.

And I had it all four years of college.

Then, I went on a trip with my girls and met Ogun.

He turned my world upside down.

What had started out as a spring break fling turned into random trips together. A year later, I was ashamed to admit that I wanted more. Foolishly, I let my feelings get involved. Ogun had given me everything I'd wanted in a situationship. I never wanted for anything. He showered me with surprise trips, gifts, and he was always honest with me... until recently.

A month ago, a picture of him and his labelmate, Lyric, had gone viral. A week passed before he addressed it, telling me not to believe everything I saw on the internet. I would've taken heed to his words if Lyric hadn't posted pictures of Ogun's tatted arm hanging over her shoulder with the eye emoji. That was when I started overthinking and became the girl I'd promised never to become.

So, for the past two weeks, I'd been ignoring him. It was childish, but I wasn't ready to face him just yet. With him locked away at his in-home studio in San Diego, I knew he was preoccupied and wouldn't have the time to question my distance.

Dating Carson was supposed to take my mind off Ogun. He should've been the distraction I needed to remind myself why I didn't do long-term connections. But the way he droned on and on made me reconsider casual dating.

By the end of the date, the conversation had shifted back to him. Somehow, we'd gotten to the past relationship portion of the evening, again. I mean, how many times did we have to talk about exes? It became redundant after the first date. Clearly, he wasn't over his last relationship. I wanted so badly to tell him to go back to her and work it out. After sharing too much information about his ex-fiancée, Carson hinted at wanting to know about my past.

"Technically, I've never been in a relationship," I admitted before taking another bite of my apple pie.

"So you've only dated? Never a serious relationship?"

While nodding my head, I continued to chew my pie.

"How long have these not serious relationships lasted?"

I shrugged. "A few months. In college, I was too busy partying and studying to focus on a relationship. Plus, my friends kept me pretty entertained with their mess."

"What about after college? You've been out for a year, right?"

A sigh fell from my lips. The only man I'd been with since graduating was Ogun, and what we had was complicated. So complicated that I barely understood our situation and couldn't explain it out loud if I tried.

Carson stared at me intently as he awaited an answer. I could've taken the easy way out and changed the subject. But I chose to be mature and honest.

"I dated someone for about a year."

"And it never got serious?" I shook my head. "Are

you looking for something serious? Or is this something temporary?" He waved his hand between us. "Because I'm not dating just to date."

I mulled over his words while eating another bite of my pie. "I don't know what I want, Carson. This is what I'm used to doing."

Carson's eyebrows furrowed and lips twisted. "I can change that if you let me."

With a smile, I averted my gaze. Thankfully, Carson caught the hint and changed the subject. We finished our dessert, and Carson paid for our meal. Once we made it to my car, there was the awkward "goodnight kiss" moment. I kissed his cheek and unlocked my car.

"Are you free next Friday?" Carson asked as he opened the door to my car.

Tilting my head to the side, I sighed. Tonight would probably be the last night I ever saw Carson. He wasn't over his ex and hadn't realized it yet. Or maybe he did and thought jumping into a new relationship would force him to move on. Either way, it wouldn't be fair for me to string him along with no real end goal for us. And technically, Ogun and I weren't done. Now, I needed to find a new gym so I wouldn't risk bumping into Carson.

"I'll let you know," I said after a moment.

He smiled, then kissed my forehead. Once I was settled inside my car, he walked to his, and I exhaled. As soon as I pulled out of my parking space, I called my girls to deliver the good news.

"I'm not seeing him again," I told them.

Everyone burst into a fit of giggles.

"Did he ask who you were voting for?" Bryana asked, incredulously. After I gave them a rundown of our date, the questions started.

"He didn't, but he made sure I knew who he was voting for." I rolled my eyes and chuckled. "Oh, and y'all's friend kept calling and texting me."

"You should call him back," Kassandra said.

Shaking my head, I said, "Nah. I'm good."

"Are you, though?" Destinee asked with a hint of amusement in her tone. "If you were, you wouldn't be going on dates with men named Carson out of spite."

Bryana and Kassandra giggled and agreed, getting another eye roll from me.

Gripping the steering wheel tighter, I replied, "I'm fine, really."

Kassandra hummed. "You know what I think? I think you caught feelings for him, and instead of admitting it, you're pushing him away."

"And that's okay because he caught feelings, too. That's why he is blowing you up, sis," Bryana chimed in.

"Exactly!" Kassandra shrieked.

"You're childish for posting that picture before your date. You knew it would get his attention. Now you're ignoring him when he calls." Destinee kissed her teeth. "You looked fine as hell, though."

Kassandra laughed, then said, "Which is why he's blowing her up! He's tryna find out who she's getting all cute for!"

"Y'all should be on my side."

"We are," Bryana said, "but you haven't even given him a chance to explain what's going on."

Destinee scoffed. "I'm not on your side. You've been living that player life for years. It's time to retire your jersey, sis."

"You get engaged one little time and now everyone needs to fall in love," I teased.

A few days after graduation, Destinee got engaged and moved to Dallas with her fiancé. Kassandra was in Atlanta with her boyfriend, Amani, who was also Ogun's little brother. Bryana was the only one who hadn't left me, but with her in nursing school, we barely hung out.

"I'm just saying, you like OG, and he likes you, too. And you know how conniving girls can be, give him a chance to explain," Destinee reasoned.

They didn't understand that I never needed an explanation for the women he surrounded himself with because it only lasted a day or so, until her. Any woman the blogs saw Ogun with, they claimed he were dating them. Most of the pictures were innocent.

This thing with Lyric was different.

Lyric was the new "it" girl in the industry. She was drop-dead gorgeous, could sing, and from what I saw on social media, everyone liked her.

I hated that I was jealous.

They'd been pictured together almost every day for the past month. I hadn't seen Ogun in two months, and with him working on his album, who knew the next time I'd see him. The gifts and calls couldn't pacify me forever. I wanted more, but I didn't know how to say it. I also wasn't prepared for his rejection.

"I'm home," I told them as I parked my car.

"Call him," Destinee said.

"It's not that easy. We have an agreement, and here I come with deeper feelings, messing everything up."

"Okay, and? Do you think if you tell him how you feel he's gonna cut you off? Girl, please," Bryana said with a scoff. "We're just on the outside looking in, but we can see that he genuinely cares about you."

If he cared, then he would've said something about the photos of him and Lyric.

I hummed, weary with our conversation. "I have to go."

Everyone groaned, then Kassandra said, "Let us know what he says!"

"Whatever," I grumbled before ending the call.

As I opened my front door, my phone started ringing. After kicking off my heels, I reached into my clutch and saw it was him again. A sigh expelled from my lips as I made my way down the hall to my bedroom.

"Another boring date," I mumbled as I unzipped my dress.

As I undressed, I decided that I wouldn't torture myself by going on dates with men I knew didn't stand a chance with me. That didn't mean I was going running back to Ogun either. Once I put on my favorite pair of cozy pajamas, I grabbed my work laptop and got into bed. If nothing else, my work would keep me busy and keep my mind off of him.

2

*L*yric smirked at me while waiting for the track to fade in. The smirk became a full-on smile before she sang the hook to our song. My gaze fell to the phone in my hand as I contemplated what to text Leslyn. Amani nudged me, his eyebrows drew together, and head tilted to the side. I put my phone in my pocket and folded my arms over my chest. As soon as I looked back up, Lyric's eyes met mine.

On the low (low)
With you (you)
No one has to know
What we do (what we do)
It stays between you and me

Keep it on the low (low)

The music faded out and my engineer, Mix, looked to me for the next move. With a shrug, I waved for Lyric to come out from the booth. I looked to Amani for his opinion, but he was too busy looking at his phone with a smile on his face. I figured he was texting Kassandra. Behind him were a few other people from my label, mostly songwriters and producers, a few of Lyric's friends, and my assistant.

"She did good," Mix said before leaning back into his seat. "Want to do another take?"

Shaking my head, I shifted my weight and watched as Lyric came toward me. We were finishing up a few songs together at my studio. For the past three weeks, we'd been locked in my house working on music together and she'd wasted no time making herself comfortable. In a tank top and leggings, she stood beside me as I leaned on the control module.

My house had been filled with people as we finished up my album. We were on schedule, and I wanted to keep it that way. I wanted to release my album and announce my next tour before the fall. I had a little under two months to get everything in order. On top of finishing up my album, Mecca and I were about to drop a mixtape together, and I had a few interviews lined up.

We needed to complete this album within the next week.

With a seductive smile, Lyric bumped my arm. "What do you think?"

To be honest, I had paid little attention to her last take. My mind was too preoccupied with something else. Mix read my mind and played it back. Everyone in the room nodded as my verse finished and the hook came in. Lyric danced and sang along. Her wavy, blonde hair brushed against my arm and I shook my head.

"This is such a vibe," she said, swaying her hips and snapping her fingers.

I nodded.

Our producers, Kameron and Jamaal, sent about ten beats over and we'd used all of them. I wasn't sure which songs would make my album and which ones Lyric would keep for hers. Right now, we were just enjoying the process. My last album wasn't my favorite; my creativity was stilted because of family issues, yet I forced myself to put something out for my fans' sake. The stress I was under seeped into my music. I took a year off and fell back in love with my music. Now my creativity was flowing again. Before, I was too busy trying to be what the industry wanted me to be. When truthfully, I didn't fit into one box. Once I found my sweet spot, I locked my team in my house until we finished my album.

"This would be a good single," Amani said, looking up from his phone. I shot him a look and he shrugged. "It's def a summer anthem. No one is trying to be boo'd up, just fuckin' and chillin'."

Mix tapped my arm, "He's right."

"See," Amani said, shooting me a grin.

"We should release it to promote both of our upcoming albums," Lyric chimed in.

I hadn't even thought about the first single.

All I could think about was *her*.

Ifemi.

Leslyn was ignoring me, and I didn't know why. That shit was driving me crazy.

"I'll think about it," I told them.

There were other songs I considered using as singles, but I valued Amani and Mix's opinions.

"I need to make a quick call," I said as I made my way to the door. Amani's eyebrows furrowed, and he nodded.

With my phone in my hand, I excused myself from the studio. It had been two weeks since I last heard from Leslyn. I was knee-deep in my album, and time had gotten away from me. Leslyn and I usually texted throughout the day. I sent her gifts every once in a while, especially on the days I missed her the most. Like today, I sent Leslyn her favorite flowers. I fully expected her to call me about them. The flowers were delivered hours ago and still nothing.

As I waited for her to answer the phone, Lyric joined me in the hall. She leaned against the wall across from me and smirked. The phone continued to ring as I did a sweep over her. If the circumstances were different, maybe Lyric and I could've fucked around. She was pretty as fuck, cool, and smart as hell. The thing about Lyric was that she knew how to use her looks to get her way. Our label CEO saw pictures of us at the club and discussed selling us as a couple. I told him I needed time to think about it.

At the time, I was trying to figure out if I wanted to do it and if so, how I would tell Leslyn. I was going through a period of growth. My sound was changing, I was getting older, and I needed a rebrand. But did I want to be with the "it" girl to make that happen? Or could I make that happen with the woman I wanted to be with? Before I could get back to them, Lyric posted pictures of us, catching the eyes of the blogs and her fans.

"Hey, you've reached Leslyn Harvey. I'm sorry I missed your ca–"

My jaw clenched as I disconnected the call.

Lyric laughed and shook her head. "Who is she?"

My eyebrow rose and I shrugged.

It was none of her business, honestly. The thing I liked most about Leslyn was her desire to stay out of the limelight. There were several times where she could've made our situation public, but she didn't. Although I had said nothing about it yet, the way Lyric was handling our upcoming collaborations irritated me.

I knew that the idea of us being together would pique our fans' interest and help with promotion and streams. However, Lyric and her team didn't check with me before going forward. So, for the past month, Lyric had posted cryptic pictures and posts about us.

The pictures and videos were childish as hell. Everyone knew the tattoos that covered my arms. Last summer, I did a spread in Rolling Stone magazine where my tatts were the focal point. Every day it seemed like a new blog was talking about us. I received texts from friends and family members about my "relationship" and the shit was exhausting. Like always, I ignored the rumors. I learned early not to give the media any energy. At the end of the day, they were going to post whatever to get engagement.

"Oh, come on. I know there's someone else. It wouldn't be you if you didn't have a few on the side."

"Nah," I grated. "You aren't my girl, Lyric. So, whoever I'm dealing with isn't *someone else.*"

"Whatever." Lyric waved her hand.

"Why are you even out here? Wassup?"

"I just wanted to talk you about everything."

I scoffed. "Why? You didn't check in before posting me in the studio last month."

"My manager told me to keep fans up to date with my projects." She pushed my arm and smiled. "You know, like behind the scenes."

"You knew what you were doing."

She took a step closer to me and grabbed the waist of my sweats.

"I don't know why Playboy OG is trying to act like a fake relationship is too much to handle. You're dating someone new like every week."

My nostrils flared as I exhaled slowly. "I'm not doing this anymore."

"We have an agreement, OG. I need this boost for my career," she pleaded.

"Yeah? I don't, though. And believe me, we don't have to sell a fake relationship for you to be successful. That shit is played out."

"You don't have to do anything. Let me be the one who is feeding the rumors."

"How do we know if this is even worth it?"

Lyric pulled her phone from her pocket and scrolled before holding the screen to my face. "You see all these DM's? These are from the picture I posted of your arm. Not only that, my streams have increased by ten percent since we hit the blogs. So, don't tell me this will not benefit me. If you have a girlfriend, I suggest you tell her what's going on and make her get on board. We need to ride this out for at least another month."

"Yeah, nah. You got a week to get whatever you need out of this, and then I'm done."

"Ogun, a week? We spend most of our time here. The paparazzi need to see us."

"A week," I said. "I'm not with this fake relationship shit, and I don't like being used. However, I don't want any bad blood between our camps since we're label-mates. Once you drop your new single, this shit is done."

"We'll need to shoot a video too, though."

Lyric pouted and tugged at the hem of my shirt.

"I don't know, man." I brushed my hand over my face. "Let's see how everything goes."

She stared at me for a moment before walking away. I stayed in the hallway a few more minutes before returning to the studio. There was no way shit between Leslyn and I would be okay after this. How was I going to explain my fake relationship with Lyric? Nothing I said would make sense because I didn't fully believe it either. It would be crazy for me to think Leslyn would understand.

I wished I'd never gotten involved with Lyric. When I met her earlier this year, I thought she was cool. We got along professionally, which was the reason our label was pushing for us to work together. Shit got a little flirtatious sometimes, but we never acted on our attraction. The more we flirted; the clingier Lyric became. Mecca tried to warn me about her, especially after being in a similar situation with Dejah a few years back. If this would've happened a year ago, I wouldn't have a problem. But now I had Leslyn's feelings to consider. Although we weren't official, I wanted us to be. She started as the homie, and over time our bond became much more.

We came into this accepting it for what it was; a situationship. When I wanted to see Leslyn, she came through, and vice versa. Now, I wanted more of her. I wanted people to know how much I adored and appreciated her. She was more than some jump-off to me. Sadly, I hadn't done a good job of letting her know just how much she meant to me. And now, I was afraid that it was too late.

Last year was rocky for us. Leslyn went through a bout of post-grad depression. Her post-grad plans hadn't panned out, leaving her working temp jobs to get by. I helped out as much as she allowed. Getting Leslyn to accept money from me was a chore. She was someone I cared for deeply, helping with her bills was the least I could do while she looked for a job.

In turn, she supported me while I was in an ongoing battle with my parents and my label. Leslyn was by my side through it all. My album didn't meet the expectations of my label. Sometimes I wanted to give up everything and duck off somewhere. Leslyn was there to remind me why I loved music. She helped me come to terms with the pain I was avoiding. We'd just become friends, and her loyalty was as strong as ever.

Last summer, my mother and I reconnected after spending most of my life estranged. With the help of my younger brother, Amani, we worked on our relationship. That came with much disapproval from my father. My parents hadn't spoken since I was twelve. I was still unaware of why they didn't last. They spent a lot of my childhood breaking up and getting back together. Once my mother had Amani, I thought they were done for good since my father was upset about her getting pregnant. During one of their breaks, she tried to make it work with Amani's father, but they broke up when he was seven. My parents tried one last time to make it work. It lasted a few years, then they called it quits for good.

All I knew was she didn't want me. After she and my father broke up for good, they sent me to Nigeria for middle and high school. The only times I came home were during the holidays. My father and I grew apart during that time because he'd gotten remarried and started a family with my stepmom. There was always a bit of jealousy toward my siblings because they'd gotten the father I'd wished I had growing up. Spending time apart from them only made my envy worse.

Upon graduation, I moved back to the states to live with him. My father had dreams of me attending an Ivy League school like he did, but that wasn't in the cards for me. While in Nigeria, I fell in love with music. I knew that when I returned to the states; I was going to pursue a career in music.

Naturally, my father disapproved. We argued about it for months before he kicked me out. Around the time of him kicking me out, I had gotten a little buzz from my first mixtape. Instead of letting my familial issues deter me from my music, I used it as motivation. The more success I had, the more tension I had with my father until the shit boiled over. Now we weren't speaking, and the shit was weighing heavily on me.

After wrapping up my sessions for the day, I sat on my deck and smoked a blunt. My eyes were low, and the agitation I felt earlier was long gone. With a grin, I looked at the starry sky. If Leslyn were here, she'd tell me where the Big and Little Dipper were. I stared at the sky, hoping I could find them. When I did, I took a picture and sent it to her.

"You good, bro?" Amani asked as he joined me on the deck.

I nodded and blew a cloud of smoke in the air. "Yup. You?"

"I'm cool. Kass is coming this weekend. I'm geeked lowkey."

With a chuckle, I replied, "I bet you are." I hit the blunt again before passing it to him.

"Talk to Les lately?"

"You already know the answer to that."

Amani hit the blunt, then laughed. "That's why you're walking around here all grouchy and shit."

"And Lyric still pushing for this fake relationship shit."

"I hate to say it, but I told you so."

My eyebrow rose. "What did you tell me?"

"That she was going to use you for clout." He sniggered and I groaned. "She's not a bad look, though," he said after putting out the blunt. "Think about it, people love seeing the next Beyoncé and Jay-Z." The glare I shot him made him laugh again. "Look, I'm just saying. You have a reputation for being a player anyway, don't you think it's time to change that narrative? Your music is changing and you're changing. Can OG settle down?"

While stroking my beard, I thought about what settling down really meant. The one person I'd trade all this shit for wasn't even speaking to me right now.

"Call Kass for me," I said after a minute.

Without question, Amani called Kassandra. "Hey, baby," he said with a smile.

"Hey. Done working for the day?"

"Yup. I'm chillin' with OG chopping it up." He handed me the phone.

"Wassup, Kass," I said, taking the phone from him.

"Hey, OG. I hope you aren't working my man too hard out there."

I shot Amani a grin. "Not at all. Listen, I wanted to know if you've talked to Leslyn lately?"

Kassandra cleared her throat. "Yeah, I have."

My eyebrows furrowed and I looked at the stars. "She cool? I haven't talked to her in a minute."

I already knew the answer. I checked her Instagram every day. Just a few days ago, she posted a picture wearing this nice ass dress, looking sexy as hell. Secretly, I hoped she was going out with her girls and not a date. The few clips she posted during her night out confirmed my fears. And I couldn't even be mad. Here I was in a whole fake ass relationship. The shit still hurt, though.

"She's okay."

"Just okay?"

Kassandra sighed. "I hoped she would've called you by now, but she saw the pictures Lyric posted. If you're with Lyric, you need to tell Les. If this is just some bullshit for the media, you need to say that, too. I'm sure she feels played."

"I understand. Between me and you, it is some bullshit for the media."

"Well, you need to be honest with Les about it. She deserves to know."

"She's not answering my calls, though, and I can't pull up on her for another two weeks."

While running my hand over my face, I sighed.

"The only thing I can say is, keep calling and keep pursuing her. The moment you stop, she'll take that as a sign to move on."

I nodded. "Aight. Thanks, Kass. See you in a few days."

After ending the call, I texted my assistant a list of gifts she needed to send Leslyn over the next week. Until I talked to her, I had some damage control to do. Once I finished this album, I was taking a few days off and visiting Leslyn. I knew I had some work to do. Leslyn deserved my full attention and penance.

3

"*A*nother special delivery for Leslyn," Alexa, my coworker, groused as she brought my package.

There were a series of gasps and moans as she made her way down the hall. My eyes closed as I prayed that Ogun didn't have an obnoxious arrangement sent to my job. The last thing I needed was my coworkers in my business. All week he'd showered me with gifts.

Meanwhile, Lyric was posting them almost every day. The pictures were mostly of his back and his arm. The picture that got to me was the one she posted this morning. Someone captured them watching the sunrise. Lyric was seated in Ogun's lap on the patio of his San Diego home.

The same home I'd visited over the last year. My stomach churned at the thought of her sleeping in his bed and walking around the house wearing the gray, cashmere robe that hung in the bathroom. Butterflies swarmed the pit of my belly as I recounted the times that I'd spent with him in the theater room, the studio, and the gym. Heat covered me as I thought of her having the same experiences tucked away in his secluded home.

Recently, they released a song together titled, "On the Low," which gave the blogs more reasons to obsess over them. I was embarrassed to say how many times I'd listened to the song. With each listen, I tried to dissect the lyrics to determine if what they had was real or not.

Alexa's footsteps grew louder, prompting me to meet her at the door of my office. After taking the flowers from her, I closed my office door. The arrangement was beautiful and made me smile. Every day for the last week, he had something delivered to me. I had three floral arrangements on my kitchen island at home, a new Chanel bag, and a Cartier LOVE bracelet to match the necklace he'd given me a while back. All the gifts overwhelmed me, along with the calls. The excitement of receiving the gifts went away after seeing him at a candlelit dinner with Lyric over the weekend.

Nothing made sense.

He called and texted me religiously, sent beautiful flowers and gifts, but he was with Lyric. The thought had me slamming the vase on my desk. As I sulked in my office, I waited for Olivia to come to my office. I instant messaged her SOS to which she replied, "Be right there."

"More goodies from 'you know who'?" Olivia, my coworker and friend, asked as she barged into my office.

"Yup," I said with a sigh. "I don't get it. He's showering me with gifts, but then I see pictures of him and Lyric all over the blogs."

Olivia frowned and took a seat on the corner of my desk. She peeked in the flowers for the card I neglected to read.

"Ifemi, I have some making up to do. See you soon." Olivia's face lit up as she jumped off my desk. "He's coming here!"

"What?" I shrieked, snatching the card from her. I read the message again and swallowed the lump in my throat.

Olivia laughed, "You in trouble, girl. I told you that you couldn't ignore him forever."

"Shut up," I sniped, making my way to the other flowers he'd sent earlier in the week. The messages varied from *call me* to *I miss you*. He'd handwritten a message for every arrangement. Now, I was curious about the flowers at home.

"You better leave early and get ready."

I scoffed. "The only thing I'm getting ready for is my date with Raphael tonight."

Last weekend, I begged Olivia and Bryana to come with me to a day party in D.C. At the party, I met Raphael. We talked for a few days before he asked me on a date. I hoped that our dates would go better than the ones I'd had with Carson. This time I was using Raphael as a distraction, I was genuinely ready to move on from Ogun. He had too much going on with him, and I wasn't about to be a part of his circus of women.

"I ain't even mad. You can't let Ogun think you're sitting around waiting for him."

"Because I'm not!"

Olivia laughed. "I have a question. If you aren't waiting for him, why did you accept the gifts and flowers?"

I shrugged. "What can I say? I like gifts," I said, laughing.

"I love it!" Olivia said, holding her hand up for a high-five.

The conversation shifted to Olivia's papers for grad school. She was still trying to convince me to get my masters, and I was still on the fence. It took months for me to get this job. Ogun listened to me cry after every denial email following a job interview. Trying to find my footing post-grad was emotionally taxing. I finally felt like I had a grip on adulthood, and I wasn't ready to jump back into school just yet.

After Olivia left my office, I went back to making graphics for our company's social media account.

Several hours later, Olivia and I strolled to the train station.

"What are you wearing tonight?" she asked as we swiped our SmarTrip cards.

I shrugged as we descended the escalator. "Probably the pink dress I sent you last week."

"Oh, yeah. That dress is super cute. Don't forget to text me when you get home. Raphael seemed cool, but you know these men be crazy sometimes."

With a chuckle, I replied, "Okay, Mom."

A few minutes later, Olivia's train arrived, and we were saying our goodbyes. As I waited for my train to arrive, I scrolled through Instagram. My eyes rolled at another post about Ogun and Lyric. The headline read, "Trouble in Paradise," and I laughed. No wonder he was heavy on the gifts this week. My train pulled up to the platform, prompting me to put in my headphones, select a playlist for the commute home, and drop my phone in my purse.

"Home sweet, home," I mused as I pulled into my complex's parking lot.

The joy I had from finally making it home went away when I saw the black Escalade double parked outside of my building. While rolling my eyes, I parked my car and grabbed my purse. I looked straight ahead, ignoring the truck as I ascended the steps. The footsteps behind me had my heart racing and blood boiling. Quickly, I opened my front door and tried to close it behind me.

"Come on, Les," Ogun pleaded with his hand

pushing the door open. He removed his black framed sunglasses that were his signature look, then peered at me.

My nostrils flared. "Why are you here?"

He took a step back and smirked. "You know why I'm here."

My stomach fluttered and pussy betrayed me.

Ogun leaned on the railing with his arms folded over his chest. My eyes roved over him and I groaned, disgusted with myself for being so turned on. From his crisp shape up to his deep umber skin and his heavy lidded, chestnut colored eyes, he was perfection. His locs were freshly twisted and in an updo, and his beard was trimmed; my favorite visual. My eyes continued roaming over him, and then I stopped when I noticed that Ogun had on the watch and bracelet he'd gotten to match my necklace. Instinctively, my fingers ran across the pendant hanging from the necklace. We continued to stare in silence.

Why did he have to come here looking so good?

Ogun's smirk became a full smile, and I smiled at the grill he had on.

"Can I come in, baby?"

"I'm baby, now?"

He chuckled. "Leslyn, you already know how I feel about you."

With my head tilted to the side, I said, "I know you've been with Lyric for almost two months."

"Let me explain that situation."

My eyebrow rose. "Go 'head."

"Can we talk about this inside? You want your neighbors knowing I'm here?"

Much to my dismay, I opened the door and let him inside. As he brushed past me, I caught a whiff of his cologne. A slow sigh fell from my lips as I dismissed the lustful thoughts that came to mind.

Like always, Ogun made himself comfortable on my couch, leaving little room for me. His arms stretched across the length of the couch with his legs spread wide, and his deep-set chestnut orbs were on me.

"Talk," I said, standing with my arms folded.

He licked his lips before smiling. "There's nothing funny, Ogun. Hurry and talk so I can get ready for my date." That replaced his smile with a scowl.

"Damn, Les. It's like that?"

"You made it this way." My arms dropped to my side as I let my anger and disappointment take over.

"You're right," he conceded. "That's why I'm here. I need to make shit right with us. The shit you saw with Lyric was just for show."

"Yeah, okay."

"For real. She needed a little boost in her music and the label thought if we faked a relationship it would help. Everything was strictly business with us."

"Why should I believe you?" I asked.

Ogun stood and reached for my hand. Gently, he pulled me to him and cupped my chin.

"Because I'm here."

I heaved a sigh as goosebumps dotted my skin from his touch. God, how I missed him. Being this close to him confused me. We had an agreement and he didn't hold up his end of the deal. I knew Ogun had a reputation, but that didn't matter to me. He always made sure I knew the truth and made sure I was secure with our situation.

Every rumor that came out, he called me and we laughed about it. Not this time. He was radio silent for weeks. I guess eventually; he figured out that I was pissed about him and Lyric, so he started damage control with gifts. Sure, he never posted pictures of him and Lyric. He never liked or commented on her posts like she did his. Still, he didn't communicate what was going on with me and that wasn't okay.

"You being here isn't enough," I said, moving from his hold.

I went to my room and closed the door. After running the shower, I undressed and got in. I prayed that by the time I got out, he would be gone. For weeks, I rehearsed what I would say when I confronted him. All that preparation went out the window when we were face to face. I was truly conflicted. Part of me wanted to forget everything that had happened and be honest with him about my feelings. The other part of me wanted to hold my ground.

When I exited the bathroom, Ogun was seated on the foot of my bed waiting for me. Gripping my towel, I walked to my dresser and grabbed my lotion. I applied the lotion with my back to him. We sat in silence, my heart racing faster with every passing second. Ogun chuckled at the bra and panty set I put on. The strapless black bra and matching thong were his favorite. If he weren't here, I wouldn't have worn it.

"Going out with Bryana?"

I stalked over to my closet and retrieved the pink bodycon dress I bought for tonight. Stepping into the dress, I pulled the spaghetti straps over my shoulders and smiled in the mirror. When I came out the closet, Ogun's eyes swept over me, sending a chill down my spine. He bit his bottom lip while shaking his head.

"Nope," I said, doing a spin for him. "I have a date."

Ogun kissed his teeth. "Stop playing with me, Les."

I smirked, pleased with the jealousy that he was exuding. "I'm not. You can have fake relationships, but I can't go on dates?"

Grabbing my hands, Ogun pulled me onto his lap. He ran his nose along my neckline before kissing it. I crossed my legs and cleared my throat.

"I should've told you sooner, but I didn't know how to, baby."

"We had an agreement," I grated. "I thought transparency was everything to you?"

Ogun gripped my thigh and sighed. With every touch, my resolve weakened. I didn't want to fight with him; I wanted him to show me how sorry he was. My body craved him in the worst way. But I knew sex would only be a temporary fix.

"It is. But shit is different now."

"It is," I whispered as his hand trailed up my thigh and under my dress.

"I knew this shit would hurt your feelings."

"Watching shit unfold on social media hurts more than you telling me. I had to jump to my own conclusions."

"You're right and I apologize for that, but you didn't even give me a chance to explain. You ignored me for weeks."

"So, you thought the gifts and flowers would make up for everything?"

"I knew you wouldn't turn down the gifts, and each one had a message. Did you read them?"

I nodded. "I read some of them, not all of them, though."

He chuckled throatily in my ear. "I figured."

"You never sent messages with gifts before."

Ogun grabbed my neck and made me face him. His lips grazed mine before curving into a smile. "Shit between us has changed. It's not just about the sex anymore."

My head fell back when his thumb found my clit. "What is it about now?"

Ogun kissed my neck and ear before saying, "It's all about you now. Whatever I need to do to prove that you're who I want, I'll do it."

Using his thumb, he ran slow circles around my clit. I melted into him and submitted to the pleasure I desperately needed.

"You think it's that easy, huh?" I asked breathlessly.

"Nah, I know you'll make me work for it."

Sliding my panties to the side, he slid two fingers

into my wetness, while still stimulating my clit. My hips moved against his hand and breaths quickened as he brought me to a much-needed climax. Using his free hand, he massaged my breasts while kissing my neck. I gripped the back of his neck and spread my legs wider.

"Let me make it up to you, baby," he crooned.

My moans grew louder, and stomach muscles tightened. Ogun's hand moved from my breast to my neck. Tilting my head to the side, he nipped and sucked my neck as I reached an intense climax. Ogun groaned as my juices covered his fingers. Once I came down from my post climactic high, he slid my panties down and held them in his hand.

"I will after my date," I told him as I rushed in the bathroom to freshen up.

When I opened the door, he was standing there, his gaze pensive.

"If you think I'm about to let you go out with some corny nigga lookin' like that, you're trippin.'"

"Let?" I asked with a laugh. "I made these plans before you ended your fake relationship." I pushed him aside and searched for the heels I wanted to wear tonight. Ogun stood behind me, his erection pressing into my backside. Pressing my lips together, I stood up and faced him. "You don't have the privilege of me cancelling plans for you anymore."

"Okay," he said, taking another step toward me, forcing me to back into the corner. "Do I still have this privilege?" he kneeled down and threw my leg over his shoulder.

Ogun's tongue swiped across my clit, making my knees buckle. I held his head for support and rocked my hips against his tongue. It wasn't long before I was panting, cursing, and gripping his hair as I came. My phone rang, snapping me out of my haze.

"Les, don't go," Ogun pleaded. His eyebrows furrowed and eyes narrowed. For a moment, I stared at him, unsure if I should give him another chance. His phone vibrated in his pocket and I rolled my eyes. He ignored the call and grabbed my waist. "Come with me, baby." His phone vibrated again and mine continued to ring. I pushed him back and ran over to the living room for my purse.

"Hello?" I answered. I held my bottom lip between my teeth as I watched Ogun remove his shirt, then jeans while walking toward me.

"I'm on my way to the restaurant. Do you need me to send the address?" Raphael asked.

Ogun stood within inches of me and dropped his boxers.

"Cancel the date," he mouthed while gripping his girthy, hardened dick.

My mouth watered at the sight of his naked body. Ogun was literal perfection from head to toe. There was no point in me denying myself the pleasure and apology I deserved.

"Actually, I can't make it tonight, something came up," I said, damn near drooling at Ogun as he stroked his dick.

I ended the call after making some excuse about

having to work late. Ogun cupped my chin and brought my lips to his. My tongue played at the seam of his lips, hungry for his. His hands went around my waist, and mine around his neck. Our mouths molded together as I melted further into his embrace. Ogun smiled against my lips before turning me around and bending me over the arm of my couch. After retrieving a condom from his jeans, he covered himself, then slid into me.

I hissed as he inched into me. In a swift motion, Ogun pulled my dress over my head and tossed it across the room. Next, he unhooked my bra and cupped my breasts.

"Damn, Les. You got me out here begging."

I moaned as he slowly stroked me. "It's what you deserve."

He chuckled, then kissed my shoulder. "Fair," he grunted. "Now let me give you what you deserve."

With a smile, I reached for a pillow to muffle my moans. The last thing I needed was for my neighbors to hear me.

4

" I never thought you would be the type to watch me sleep," Leslyn said while stretching.

Running my hand over my face, I laughed. She was right. I wasn't the type to do corny shit like that. But I couldn't help myself. Leslyn was sleeping so peacefully and looked so angelic. And I was grateful she was giving me a chance to make up for the last two months.

Last night, we checked in at The Dupont Circle for the weekend. Leslyn was mine for the next three days and I was going to make it worth her while. She made it clear that my words meant nothing. By the end of the weekend, she was going to know how much she meant to me.

My eyes followed her as she tiptoed to the bathroom. I'd always loved her long, smooth, almond brown colored legs. While she took care of her morning hygiene, I ordered us breakfast. Since I wanted to surprise her, I ordered everything off the menu. I also ordered two bottles of champagne, along with orange and mango juice.

By the time she finished up in the bathroom, I had switched gears to work. Amani sent me a few tracks from the album to listen to and critique. My brother had been working just as hard as I was on this album. Just as I was growing as an artist, he was too. Amani had a signature sound, and he knew how to make me and the music one. Not only was he more confident, he'd even branched out and started working with other people.

"What are you working on now?" Leslyn asked, taking a seat next to me on the couch.

I took off my headphones and put them over her ears. She nodded as the track played back. With a grin, she stared at me. Those damn maple colored eyes had me grinning right back. When I tried to stop the song, she grabbed my hand, then shook her head. I looked at the computer to see the name of the track. My stomach knotted when I realized she was listening to the song I wrote about her. In my mind, I'd planned out this extravagant way to play the song for her. The longer she stared, the more vulnerable I felt.

And I hated that shit.

Leslyn came into my life and stole my heart.

It was unexpected, but necessary.

Just a year ago, I was teasing Amani for falling in love with Kassandra. When I met Leslyn and her friends, I expected us to kick it a few times and lose contact. That's how it always went. There were no complaints from either party once the situation ended. Not with Leslyn, though. We went from only talking when I wanted to fly her out to talking every day. I was making space for her in my life.

The shit happened so subtly that neither of us had time to address it. I just knew I liked the shift between us. Then came the feelings, the shit I tucked away and never wanted to show. The trips became more frequent and the gifts did, too. Neither of us had ever been in a long-term relationship. This shit was new to us and admittedly, I was afraid that an official title would make things complicated.

The only thing that complicated us was my inability to open up to her.

So, I wrote "Ifemi" and rapped all the words I was afraid to say to her.

Once the song ended, Leslyn removed the headphones. "It's beautiful."

"This wasn't how I wanted you to hear the song."

She smiled softly. "Why couldn't we just say how we felt?"

"I wish I knew, but that's why I'm here now," I said, reaching for her hand.

Leslyn sighed. "We do this all the time." She looked around the suite with furrowed eyebrows. "What's so different now? Come Monday, I'll be back at work, and you'll be on the blogs pictured with someone else." She removed her hand from mine and walked over to the balcony door.

"Nah, that's not happening."

"How do you know?"

I walked over to her and wrapped my hands around her waist. "Because come Monday, you'll be my woman, and there won't be any further confusion."

"Yeah, okay," Leslyn said with a laugh.

I kissed her neck, turning her laugh into a moan as she settled in my embrace. Just as I untied her robe, our breakfast arrived. Leslyn watched with wide eyes as the servers rolled in four trays of food and drink. After tipping everyone, I uncovered everything and popped a bottle of champagne.

"We're not going to finish all this food, OG." I smirked as she tried to fill her plates with a little of everything. "But I mean, I can try." She laughed.

"Don't eat too much. We have massages scheduled in two hours."

Leslyn tossed her head back while chewing her food. After swallowing, she said, "I need a massage so bad. I can't wait."

It had been a while since we'd gotten massages. The last time we linked up, I had a personal masseuse come to my house. I'd just gotten off tour and needed to recharge. The only person I wanted to spend time with was Leslyn. I flew her out Friday night, and for the weekend, I pampered us. We had a chef come and cook for us every night, went shopping, and watched movies in my theater. After that weekend, I started working on my new album. We knew we'd see less of each other, and I thought I was prepared for it until I had to drop her off at the airport. I hugged her a little longer, kissed a little sweeter, and lingered longer as she made her way to check in.

After finishing breakfast, I showered and dressed casually in a pair of sweats and a t-shirt. Leslyn had gotten dressed while I showered. She wore a similar outfit as she sat on the balcony.

"The car will be here in a few," I told her as I stepped outside.

Leslyn faced me. While handing me her phone, she said, "You're officially single."

On her screen was a selfie of Lyric with the caption, "Single AF!" I chuckled while handing Leslyn back her phone.

"The comments are saying it's your fault, you cheated on her, and that she used you for clout. The last one is my personal favorite."

Taking a seat next to her, I said, "Good thing they'll never know the truth, huh?"

"Did you like her?"

"Nah. Lyric is cool peoples. She's definitely a schemer and will do whatever it takes to make it. For that alone, I could never be more than an associate to her. The woman I like and want is right here."

Leslyn's cheeks turned red as she replied, "So why'd you do it? If I'm the one you want so badly?"

"Lyric got tired of waiting for me to give her an answer, so she started posting pictures. In hindsight, I should've said something sooner. To her, then you. I shouldn't have had you out here unsure of your position in my life."

Leslyn's eyes darkened and lips twisted. "The car will be here any minute. We need to head downstairs," she mumbled, then rushed inside.

I wanted to chase after her and finish our conversation but decided against it. She was retreating and I couldn't blame her. To her, I was like the other men she'd dealt with in the past.

We rode to the spa in silence. Leslyn kept busy by scrolling through social media, while I was fixated on her. My eyes skated over her soft features. Her lips curved into a smile as her fingers moved swiftly across the phone screen. When she looked up and caught my gaze, her smile fell. This was why I hated when feelings got involved. Before, we could kick it without fighting or tension.

Once we reached our destination, Leslyn entered the spa first and I followed behind. After checking in, we undressed and put on our robes. Between the lavender essential oil and the calm music playing, I was ready to fall asleep. The hour-long couple's massage loosened the tension between us. As we waited to enter the sauna, Leslyn held my arm. I peered down at her and smiled.

"Are we friends again?" I asked, getting a smile from her.

"I think we're past that point."

"We are." I stared at her knowingly.

Our hostess returned with fresh towels and led us to our personal sauna. We changed out of our robes and into our towels before taking a seat. Leslyn sat across the sauna from me. All I could do was chuckle. It took a few minutes for the steam to fill the room. I leaned back and exhaled. My body was at ease, finally. The late nights and crazy schedule had caught up to me. There was no one I'd rather decompress with than her.

I lifted my head and nodded for Leslyn to come to me. She rolled her eyes before standing. While holding her towel, she sat next to me. Leslyn's almond colored skin was covered in a sheen of sweat. I grabbed the nape of her neck, then tugged the loose curl that was stuck to her skin. While licking my lips, I moved closer to her. Leslyn sighed as I ran my hand up her thigh and under her towel.

"What do I need to do to regain your trust?"

"Be honest and consistent," she breathed

"I can do that," I said truthfully. My hand inched further under her towel. A smile covered my mouth when she spread her legs open for me.

"You talk a good game, OG." She moved my hand and closed her legs. "But let's be honest, you don't want to be in a relationship."

"If you're scared, just say that. But don't flip this

back on me. I'm trying to show you how serious I am about us. You gotta let your guard down, baby."

Leslyn's eyebrows met and eyes narrowed. "Easy for you to say. I have more to lose in this situation than you."

"Nah. We're both out here wide open and vulnerable as hell." Leslyn grew quiet as she mulled over my words. I let a few seconds tick by before saying, "Now, come here and give me a kiss."

She smiled, then leaned in, capturing my lips with hers. Gripping her by the neck, I tilted her head back to kiss her neck. Leslyn grabbed my hand and moaned as I trailed kisses down her neck to her chest. Gently, I leaned forward until I was on top of her. After opening her towel, I untied her bikini top and sucked one nipple while tweaking the other. Her back arched from the bench as I wrapped my arm around her waist. Continuing my pursuit to please her, I dropped kisses down to her stomach. Without instruction, she spread her legs wide for me. Then, she raised her hips for me to remove her bottoms.

I slid my finger over her slippery folds and spread them apart. My mouth landed on her clit and I immediately went to work. With each lick and suck, the louder Leslyn's moan grew. Her nails dug into my shoulders and I smiled in her pussy. Kissing her inner thighs, I wrapped my arms around them to scoot her closer to me. I looked up and caught her lusty gaze.

"Les, tell me it's mine," I ordered before latching on to her clit.

She attempted to answer, her words coming out as moans and curses. I continued to devour her sweet spot while inserting two fingers inside her. Curving my finger just right, I hit the right spot, making her peak inevitable. Her warm juices covered my lips, and I caught every drop.

"It's yours, Ogun," she moaned while grabbing my shoulders.

I brought my mouth to hers for a wet, sloppy kiss. Leslyn sucked my bottom lip and tongue while I eased in her.

"Wait," she said, pressing her hand against my chest. "Someone could walk in."

"No one is coming in here," I assured her.

The owner of this spa's son was a fan of mine. After meeting them at a meet and greet last fall, he left me his card and promised me the best the next time I was in town. When I planned my weekend visit, I called in on that favor.

Leslyn studied me for a moment before removing her hand from my chest. Her eyes closed as I moved my hips. I did the same while tilting my head back and biting my bottom lip. She was so wet and warm, and just as good as I remembered. Leslyn's nails dug into my flesh when I picked up my strokes. Leaning down, I captured her mouth with mine. I swallowed every moan she expelled while trying to hold back my own. She giggled and sucked my bottom lip, knowing it would push me over the edge.

"I missed you," she confessed while peering at me through low eyes.

"I missed you too, baby."

Raking her hands through my beard, Leslyn brought my lips back to hers. I continued to rock into her steadily as we took our time tasting each other. Our kiss became heated as I stroked her harder and her moans grew louder. Our gazes locked on to each other's as we fell down into an abyss of inexplicable pleasure.

After we cleaned ourselves, we left the sauna and showered.

"What's next," she asked, gathering her bag and shoes

"City Center."

Leslyn nodded with a smile.

She loved shopping at City Center. There were a few pieces I wanted from the Hermes store and there was no one I was more willing to drop a bag on than Leslyn.

5

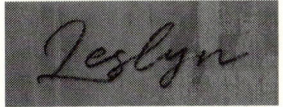

I was overwhelmed, but in a good way.

Ogun's presence made me feel exhilarated, calm, and yet somehow, I was more confused than ever about what I wanted. After accidentally listening to the song he'd written for me, it made sense why he showered me with gifts.

Aside from the song, he wasn't sure how to express his feelings for me. So instead of telling me, he was trying his hardest to show me. Now, I was afraid that I wouldn't be able to live up to the expectations he had for me.

I knew for sure I wanted him. There hadn't been a man that made me feel like this ever. And he had said the same about me. But could I love Ogun the way he deserved? I'd been selfish and self-centered much of my adult life; my needs came before anyone else's. I barely knew how to deal with the conflict between us. The first time I saw Ogun and Lyric, I retreated instead of confronting him. The thought of losing him hurt more than I cared to admit.

Ogun tugged my arm and smiled at the display before us. The next activity on our list was shopping. Typically, he'd buy me whatever and have it sent to me. But today, he wanted to take me shopping.

"Which ones do you want?" he asked, peering at the display of bracelets, necklaces, and rings.

What woman didn't want to hear that question?

"Um," I said, staring at the TIFFANY & CO sign straight ahead, then back at the display case. "I like the butterfly necklace and bracelet."

"I figured." He ran his thumb across the butterfly tattoo I had on my wrist. A smile formed on the corners of my lips. "What else do you want?"

The clerk smiled. "We also have this butterfly necklace," she said, unlocking the display. Once she retrieved the necklace, she placed it softly on her palm. A gasp fell from my lips and my eyes widened.

"We'll take this one, too," Ogun said with a nod. He pressed a kiss on my temple, sending a wave of warmth over me.

The clerk smirked before disappearing in the back to get our items. I glanced around the pristine showroom in awe. It was every woman's dream to shop at Tiffany's, and I was living it.

"This is too much," I muttered, catching Ogun's attention.

"Yet, I feel like it's not enough." He snaked his arm around my waist, drawing me closer to him. I fought the urge to smile at the feeling of simply being this close to him. A whiff of his cologne filled my nostrils and I exhaled in delight.

"I don't need all this," I said, honestly.

Ogun's eyebrows furrowed as he licked his lips. "Tell me what you need then?"

My stomach fluttered and pussy pulsated. His heavy gaze met mine. Swallowing the lump in my throat, I answered him, "Consistency."

"I'm working on that. What else?"

"Security."

"What does that look like for you?"

I shrugged while chewing my bottom lip. "Acknowledgement, I guess. I need to know that there isn't a woman who could take my place."

"Trust me, it's known, baby."

My eyebrow rose and he continued, "Lyric knows about you. That's why I never came out and confirmed us. And you're why I never even kissed her. I don't want her, or anyone else for that matter." Ogun ran his hand over his face and looked around. Aside from us, the only people here were the store's security and Ogun's security.

"Mhm," I teased with a laugh, trying to lighten the

mood. Ogun had switched up and gotten serious on me.

He gripped my waist tighter and leaned down to my ear. "You want me? You have me. My heart is yours, baby. All the bullshit before this moment means nothing to me. Hopefully soon, you can say the same for me."

My mouth fell agape, and heart pounded against my chest. My only saving grace was the call he received. "You should get that," I told him. Ogun smirked knowingly before releasing me from his hold.

He nodded toward the door and his security guard followed him. While Ogun took his call, I moseyed around the store and admired all the jewelry. The clerk returned with five Tiffany blue boxes and waved for me to come to the counter.

"My…" I stopped, unsure of what to call Ogun. "Ogun had to step out to make a call."

She nodded, then rang up our items. "What's the special occasion?" she asked, bagging the items.

"I'm sorry?" I replied with furrowed eyebrows.

"Is it your birthday? An anniversary?"

Shaking my head, I said, "Just because."

The clerk smiled. "My favorite occasion."

I returned the smile before looking over my shoulder. "It's becoming my favorite, too."

The door chimed and in came Ogun. His smile from earlier was gone. "How much?"

He handed the clerk his card before she could tell him the total.

Instinctively, I reached for his hand to comfort him. I learned that was the quickest way to calm him down. This past summer, Ogun wanted to reconcile with his parents and needed my support in both instances. After meeting my parents, Ogun shared the issues he and his parents had with me.

We started with his mother since they were at the point where they wanted to fix things. They went to dinner and talked. Afterward, Ogun and his mother worked to repair their relationship. It took a little more work with his father. Once Ogun finally got his father to agree to meeting him, Ogun asked me to come too. Initially, I was stunned and felt my presence was inappropriate. He didn't see it that way. So, I went and realized why he needed me there.

Ogun was one of the most confident and headstrong men I knew. But when he came face to face with his father, he was unsure of himself and meek. Whenever the conversation got intense, I'd hold his arm. From just my touch, he could center himself and focus. The dinner didn't end the same way it had with his mother, but it was a start.

Later that night, he told me he'd brought me for support, and to prove to his father he could have a healthy relationship with a woman. Apparently, another issue between them was Ogun's reputation and history with women.

As gently as he could, he expressed that I was the closest to a girlfriend that he'd ever had. That night was the first time I felt we could be more. Over time, I found reasons to negate the fact that I wanted more than a fuck buddy. And now here we were, facing the inevitable, and it scared me shitless.

After making a few more purchases, we went back to the hotel. Ogun was still visibly frustrated. I tried to give him some space to sort through whatever he was going through. As I organized the bags from today's shopping spree, Ogun ran the shower and undressed. I turned around just as he pulled his t-shirt over his head. My mouth watered at the sight of his deep umber chest that was covered in tattoos. He caught me staring at him and smirked. I took that as an opportunity to ask what was wrong.

"You okay?" I asked and pressed my hands into his abs. I took my time running my hands down his chest until I reached the waist of his joggers.

"I'm cool," he replied, grabbing my waist and licking his lips. "I'm glad you're here with me. The last few weeks have been stressful as fuck."

"I'm happy to be here with you, too." Slowly, I tilted my head back. He brushed his lips against mine before looking at me. "You wanna tell me why your mood changed after that phone call?"

He eyed me for a minute before dropping his hands from my waist. Mine remained firmly on his waist as I awaited his response.

"Lyric wants me to be in the video for 'On the Low' after we agreed that I wouldn't."

"Oh," I said. "Are you going to do it?"

"I don't want to, but my manager's all like 'it's your

song too' and 'it'll prove the breakup was amicable.' Which is just his wife, who works in PR, talking."

"I mean," I drawled.

Ogun groaned. "I told her to do it without me and she agreed to doing the video without me. This woman is determined to be a pain in my ass."

"Seems like she really likes you." I took a step back as I tried to make my way back to my things. Ogun grabbed my wrist, keeping me within his reach.

"Yeah, and she was probably hoping I'd eventually like her too, but nah." His chestnut orbs narrowed, and he took a step toward me.

"Yeah," I pushed out, too caught up in the look in his eye. "So, what are you gonna do?"

He shrugged, then pulled down his joggers. "I'm not thinking about that right now."

My eyes dropped to the bulge in his underwear as I bit my bottom lip. "What are you thinking about?"

"You. Always you."

Ogun cupped my ass and pulled me toward him. My hands rested on his chest as his lips came crashing into mine. Ogun's kisses were truly a drug. As I pressed up on my toes to deepen our kiss, his tongue met mine. The throaty groans he elicited had me melting into him as I wrapped my arms around his neck.

"How much time do we have before dinner?" I asked while he kissed my neck.

"An hour and a half," he answered hastily before returning his kiss to mine. Ogun guided me toward the steamy shower and ended our kiss to undress me. "Damn, Les," he growled, gripping his dick.

My cheeks warmed as I stood before him. After putting my hair in a messy bun, I reached for his hand as I backed into the shower. Ogun smirked as he approached me with fire in his eyes. The warm water sprinkled over me as I backed into a corner, my sights set on Ogun's lips.

Seemed like he had the same idea, grabbing my neck to angle my head enough to meet his hungry mouth. His thumb rested on my voice box as he nipped and sucked my bottom lip until it numbed. Once he got his fill, he dropped his hand from my neck to hoist me up. I moaned when he slid into me.

"Don't drop them legs," he ordered, making me wrap my legs around his waist as best as I could.

My back slid against the tiled shower wall with every thrust. Ogun's grunts and hard, steady strokes were too much, sending me into a state of euphoric pleasure. My nails dug into his shoulders as he firmly gripped my ass. Ogun pulled back and looked at me. He planted one hand on the wall while the other held my waist.

"What?" I asked, slightly self-conscious.

"You're so fucking beautiful, Les," he answered, slowing his strokes down before ejecting from me.

Releasing my legs, Ogun led me to the bench on the opposite side of the shower. He sat down and grinned as I straddled his lap. We hissed as I rocked in a steady motion. Our eyes locked, his gaze heated and vulnerable. He sat in a daze with his bottom lip between his teeth. I smirked and moved my hips faster. Ogun sat up, smacked my ass and nodded in approval before kissing me passionately. My head fell back, and I held his head as he kissed and sucked my breasts.

When a familiar sensation came over me, I released Ogun and used his thighs to brace myself. Rocking faster, I welcomed an intense orgasm. Through heavy lids, I saw Ogun's grin as he reached between my legs, heightening my experience.

"That's it, baby," he coached as my juices covered him.

I'd barely come down from my high before he held my waist, leaning forward, delivering intoxicating, debilitating strokes that had my eyes rolling back. A few minutes later, he was grunting curses as he pulled out of me and spilled his seeds on the shower floor.

Ogun stood under the water, beckoning me with a nod. I shook my head, not wanting to get my hair wet.

"Com'ere, baby."

With a smile, I shook my head again.

"Damn, you 'bout to make me beg again?"

"Maybe."

He smirked and met me halfway for an ardent kiss. At this rate, we would never make it to dinner.

———

"*Y*ou always outdo yourself," I said as Ogun pushed my chair to the table.

He winked in response before taking a seat across from me. We barely made our reservation, but thanks to Ogun's gift of gab, we could still sit in the private room he reserved for us. As we waited for our server, I looked around the room in awe.

The Palma room was next to the restaurant's wine cellar that we would tour after dinner. The walls were dark teal with abstract painting adorning the walls. The intimate lighting added to the room's romantic aesthetic. I wondered if this was how it always looked or if Ogun had requested this. Behind me was a panoramic window that overlooked the Potomac River. I was so busy admiring the view that I hadn't noticed our sommelier had entered the room. After giving us a list of suggestions, we settled on two bottles and ordered appetizers.

Once we were alone, Ogun stood from the table and waited for me to do the same. He held out his hand for mine and walked us over to the window. Standing behind me, his hands rested on my waist. I took a deep breath, relishing in his embrace and the delicious scent of his cologne mixed with weed.

"The view is beautiful," I mused, settling into his embrace.

"It is. Before I met you, I'd probably been to D.C. a handful of times. It was always on some tourist shit, so I never enjoyed myself."

"That's funny because I've been here my whole life and never toured the city."

Ogun chuckled. "My father is obsessed with American history. We've been here, Mount Rushmore, fucking Gettysburg, and we toured the south to learn about the Civil Rights Movement. Whenever I came home from Nigeria, he had an itinerary of shit for us to do, until he remarried."

"Maybe you should plan a trip to the Grand Canyon or something. I remember you saying he likes nature and being outdoors," I suggested after hearing the nostalgia in his voice.

"Nah, it's not the same now."

"Well, you won't know until you try." I turned to face him.

"Always the optimist," he said, then kissed my forehead.

I couldn't help the smile on my face as I raised my chin for a kiss. Ogun granted my wish, bringing his soft, full lips to mine. For seconds we lost ourselves in the warmth of our kiss. My arms went around his neck, and his the small of my back. Ogun's kisses were like a drug. There was never a such thing as too many. Eventually, Ogun pulled back, ending our kiss and leaving me longing for more.

With a sigh, he asked, "So, wassup, Leslyn?"

My eyebrows met as I responded, "What do you mean?"

I tried to move from his hold, but he only held me tighter. Our bodies pressed firmly together as I bored into his chestnut orbs. I knew what he was asking, but I didn't have the answer.

"Us," he stated, simply. His baritone sent a chill down my spine.

Luckily, the sommelier saved me from having to answer. We returned to the table and waited for our appetizers to arrive. I sipped my wine and moaned at the notes of cherry in my pinot noir. The waiter came a few moments later with our Ibiza seafood tower, which was an assortment of oysters, prawns, tuna, lobster and mussels.

"This food is bomb," I said, chewing a piece of tuna. It paired perfectly with our wine.

Ogun nodded with a smile. He held a prawn over the table for me to take a bite. I covered my mouth as I chewed my food. Next, he fed me an oyster, gently brushing his thumb across my bottom lip in the process. He continued to feed me until the waiter returned, ready to take our entrée orders.

Across the table, Ogun stared at me with curious eyes. A part of me wanted to ask what was on his mind, the other part of me knew already. He wanted answers. He wanted me to take charge and put a label on us, and I just couldn't. I wasn't ready for all that came with being in a relationship. Things would change between us. No matter how hard we tried, things would change.

"When I first saw you at that club in Miami, I never thought we'd be here today. We spent the week kickin' it and gettin' to know each other, and I was cool with that. I needed that. I know I have a rep for being a hoe and out there, partly because it's true," he said with a chuckle.

"But you helped me to slow down and get my life back on track. I was caught up in that celebrity shit and almost lost myself. I don't need a slew of women in my bed and my face to feel like a man. I needed stability, loyalty, a friend. That's everything you've been for me. The trips and time we spend together only make my feelings for you deeper. The whole shit with Lyric was the first time I felt like I could lose you, and that... fucked me up."

"Aren't you afraid of everything changing?" I asked.

He shrugged easily and said, "Change can be good sometime, baby." For a moment, he assessed me. Then, he chuckled before taking a sip of wine. "I go back to San Diego in two days and I don't want to go back home wondering how much longer we'll play this game."

"Game?"

"Yeah, the one where we act like we aren't falling for each other. The one where we act like fuckin' is just enough." He stared at me steadily, though his tone conveyed annoyance and disappointment, even. A beat passed before he sighed and leaned back in his seat.

I did the same, reaching for my glass to gulp down the rest of my wine.

"I'm afraid, okay?"

"Of what?"

"Not being good enough for you." I held up my hands. "I can't compete with this," I said, looking around the private room.

"I'm not asking you to. This is how I show you I care. You told me a man never went out of his way for you before, so I did. I send gifts because I remember the way your face lit up the first time I got you those diamond earrings in your ears. Les, I already told you what I needed and how you fulfilled those needs for the past year."

While swallowing the lump in my throat, I adjusted in my seat. The waiter entered the room with a cart of food, saving me from having to respond. After he set everything down and left, Ogun changed the subject to his upcoming album release. Though I was relived we were talking about something less intense, I hoped my inability to open my heart didn't ruin our last day together.

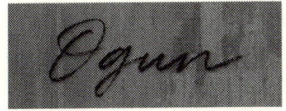

6

"__H__ave you thought about what we discussed yesterday?" David, my manager, asked.

I groaned before averting my gaze to Leslyn, who was sitting on the couch eating a bagel and talking on the phone.

"Look, I know this situation wasn't ideal, but it was beneficial to the both of you," he persisted.

"David, I ain't tryna hear all that. A few thousand followers and streams hardly mean it was beneficial."

He chuckled. "I get it, I do. But this is business."

"Business I should've never gotten involved in."

"I'll tell them you need a few more days to decide. They want to shoot Friday, so they'll need an answer soon. Make sure you check out the treatment. Tell Leslyn I said hello."

"See you tomorrow."

I sighed and dropped my phone on the nightstand. Tomorrow, I was heading back to San Diego, and I wasn't looking forward to it. Especially since shit between me and Leslyn was still unresolved.

Leslyn ended her call when she saw me coming her way.

"What's the plan for today?" she asked with a smile. After patting the space next to her, she handed me a bagel.

I knew Sundays were usually reserved for her parents. We slept through church, but I knew her mother would cook tonight, and I couldn't remember the last time I'd had a home cooked meal.

"Dinner with your folks."

Her eyebrows shot up and eyes widened. "You really want to spend our last day with my parents?"

"Yeah, why not? I don't want to mess up your ritual with them."

I met her parents at her graduation cookout. Back then, I was just a friend she'd met a few months prior. Now, her parents knew there was something going on between us. Leslyn's mother was especially interested in what we were doing. Apparently, I was the reason Leslyn had missed too many Sunday dinners. Had I known how important they were to them; I would've been more mindful of the surprise trips I planned for us.

"I didn't tell them you were in town. They'll be happy to see you."

I smiled because I looked forward to seeing them, too. Leslyn was their world. Her father made sure that I knew it too. They weren't always close, but once they got past their issues, everything had been smooth sailing. I admired and envied their close bond. It seemed like I would never have a peaceful relationship with my parents. I knew it was a work in progress, but at times it felt like I was the only one actively trying.

Shaking away my thoughts, I met Leslyn's heavy gaze. She sighed and reached for my hand.

"About last night," she said with a sigh.

"It's cool," I interjected.

Despite how dinner ended, I still had a good time. And was still having a good time with Leslyn. She wasn't ready to let her guard down yet, and though it bruised my ego, I understood why. Our fear of getting hurt had forged our bond. Although neither of us had ever been in anything serious, we'd been in situations where we put our feelings on the line and ended up with nothing. I wasn't supposed to fall for her. I shouldn't want more than she had already given me, but I did. Now I realized that she may not be ready yet.

After dinner, we sat on the balcony and shared a bottle of champagne. We kept the conversation light. The tension between us made it impossible for me to talk to her. So, my answers were quick, and attention was elsewhere. Eventually, she gave up and silence fell over us. A few minutes passed before she headed inside to take a call. While she was on the phone, I undressed and waited for her to join me in bed. Another hour passed before she came. By the time she made it to bed, I just wanted to hold her until we drifted off to sleep.

The somber expression on her face prompted me to sit up straight.

"Destinee thinks Aubrey is cheating on her." The disappointment in her tone made me sigh. "She's devastated," she added as she settled under the covers.

I raised my arm for her to nestle under. With her hand resting on my chest, she wrapped her leg around mine. "I mean, Aubrey wasn't my first choice for her. He seemed a little controlling and immature, but Destinee loved him. She uprooted her life and moved in with him. It doesn't matter how much you do or how hard you love someone; they still fuck you over."

I pulled her closer to me as she continued to vent. Part of me knew she was just expressing her disappointment in her friend's situation. I also knew that she would use this as a reason for us to keep things between us as they were. Now wasn't the time to talk about that. Instead, I listened to her. Eventually she fell asleep and shortly after; I did the same.

I guess she thought I was upset with her because when she woke up this morning, I was on the balcony. When I was really annoyed by the emails and texts I'd gotten from my manager, David.

This was the first time we'd spoken today.

Leslyn shook her head. "No, it's not. I let Destinee's

situation get to me and last night we went to bed in a weird place."

"We're good." She didn't seem convinced, so I continued, "It's our last day together and I'm not trying to ruin it. Let's go to your parents and enjoy dinner."

"Okay," she mumbled before storming over to her bags. After sifting through her duffle, she zipped it and we made our way downstairs to check out the hotel.

I wasn't in the mood for another heavy conversation. There were other things I had to worry about. Tomorrow, I would be back in grind mode. I let my personal shit affect my last album, including the promo run; and I refused to let it happen again. Whatever happened between us after this weekend, I would have to accept it.

An hour later, we pulled up to her parents' home. Against Leslyn's wishes, we went back to her apartment to get her car. It didn't seem right pulling up to her folks' house with a driver. To them, I wasn't Ogun the rapper. I was "Johanna's friend". Once she parked, we exited the car and walked down the brick path to the front door. Leslyn's mouth curved into a smile when her mother opened the door.

"Jo-Jo," her mother shrieked, then pulled her into a tight hug. I stood back with a smirk on my face. "Why didn't you tell me Ogun would be here earlier? I would've made him a pineapple upside down cake!"

Mrs. Harvey pushed Leslyn aside and reached for me.

"Yeah, Jo-Jo," I teased Leslyn, calling her by her middle name.

The first time I came to dinner, it caught me off guard hearing Leslyn's parents call her by her middle name. I had convinced myself that she gave me a fake name when we met. Luckily, her mother shared why they called her Johanna. Apparently, her middle name was supposed to be Leslyn, but at the last minute they changed it, and regretted it.

"Anyway," Leslyn drawled and pushed my arm, "I found out at the last minute."

Our eyes met and a faint grin rested on her mouth. "It's my fault," I said, my eyes still on her. "This trip was kind of a surprise."

Mrs. Harvey smiled warmly and closed the front door. "Either way, there is plenty of food and you know you're always welcomed here."

As we made our way to the living room, I handed Mrs. Harvey the bottle of whisky I'd gotten for Mr. Harvey. I knew that after dinner he would want to smoke a cigar and have a drink. Leslyn reached for my hand as we rounded the corner and smiled. Although she had yet to say it, I knew me spending time with her people meant a lot to her. There were a few times that I invited her friends on trips with us, and the joy she felt was undeniable. Mr. Harvey's face lit up when we entered the room. After sharing a long hug with Leslyn, he hugged me too.

"He brought you a gift," Mrs. Harvey said, holding up the bottle of whisky.

Mr. Harvey patted me on the back. "This is why we like you."

Leslyn scoffed and disappeared in the kitchen with her mother.

I took off my jacket and got comfortable on the couch. While Mr. Harvey watched the highlights from today's games, I checked my email hoping there was a new video treatment from Lyric's team. The original treatment had too many scenes with us. One in particular where she would give me a lap dance while I rapped my verse. I wanted to have no scenes with Lyric, but I knew that wasn't realistic.

After hearing that she did an Instagram live Q & A and addressed our fake relationship as not being completely over, I wanted nothing to do with her.

Once I saw there were no new emails from her team, I locked my phone and put it in my pocket. Mr. Harvey's attention was on the TV screen, but he pointed my way, catching my attention.

"What have you been up to?" he asked, with his eyebrows furrowed.

I shrugged. "Just finished my album and getting ready to tour again in a few months, hopefully."

"Always working," he said with a chuckle.

"I'm tryna get like you." I nodded toward the recliner, then at the TV. "I have to work a few more years before I can sit back and relax like you."

He looked at me and smiled. "Keep working as hard as are and you won't have to work much longer. But remember to take time for yourself." He paused and looked toward the kitchen. "And continue to make time for your loved ones, too."

Leslyn entered the living room with a raised eyebrow and her arms folded. When my gaze met hers, I winked. Seeing her visibly flustered from just a wink made me chuckle.

"Dinner is ready," she said, then left.

"It's grub time," Mr. Harvey mused as he stood from his recliner chair.

I used the guest bathroom to wash my hands, then joined everyone in the kitchen. Leslyn liked to eat Sunday dinner at the small table in the kitchen. She always said the dining room was too formal and too big for just the three of them.

Mrs. Harvey blessed the food and thanked the man upstairs for bringing us together again. I peeped the smile on Leslyn's lips when Mrs. Harvey said it, too. When the blessing was complete, I looked at my plate and said an extra thanks for this meal.

"I'm sure you haven't had a real home-cooked meal in a while," Mrs. Harvey said proudly.

"Ma, he has a chef," Leslyn replied while rolling her eyes.

Mrs. Harvey groaned. "Now, you know that chef is probably making those healthy flavorless meals."

I watched their exchange while chewing my food. After swallowing, I replied, "I haven't had a home-cooked meal in months. Thank you."

Leslyn kissed her teeth while Mrs. Harvey smiled. Like always, dinner was easygoing. Leslyn's parents asked her about work, and she told them about every project she was working on. Mr. Harvey took time to offer her some solid advice when she mentioned being stressed out. I sat back and watched her interact with her parents. They made me want to call mine and have them come earlier than planned.

Soon the attention shifted back to me as I told them about my tentative schedule for the rest of the year. The next month was dedicated to promoting the album with slight breaks in between. I knew that after the album dropped, I'd be going nonstop. Once again, Mr. Harvey stressed the importance of spending time with my family. I nodded, taking heed to his words. There wasn't a man whose wisdom I valued more than Mr. Harvey's.

After dinner, Mrs. Harvey took our plates and brought out a peach cobbler. I sighed, knowing I was way off my diet plan. But fuck it, I rarely ate sweets. The conversation remained light, mostly talk about current events, my music, and Leslyn's friends. Mrs. Harvey used the update on Kassandra and Amani as a segue into asking about me and Leslyn's situation.

"So, what are y'all doing?" she asked innocently before filling her mouth with a piece of cobbler.

"Ma!" Leslyn shrieked.

"Johanna!" Mrs. Harvey shot back.

"Please, don't start this."

"What? He's the first man you've ever brought home. And he's been around for over a year now."

Leslyn shot her mother a glare that made Mrs.

Harvey drop the subject. A few minutes passed before Mrs. Harvey excused herself and Leslyn followed. When the ladies left, Mr. Harvey let out a chuckle.

"Ready for that cigar?" he asked, pushing his chair from the table.

I nodded, eager for some fresh air and a glass of whisky.

———

"How are your parents?" Mr. Harvey asked, then took a pull from his cigar.

After taking a gulp of my drink, I replied, "They're good. I'm thinking about asking them to come a few days before my album release party. I need to spend some one-on-one time with them. The only time I ever spend with them is when I have an event."

"Yeah, do that. I know things are still rocky, but they can't say you aren't trying."

I nodded. The first time Leslyn brought me to dinner at her parents, Mr. Harvey asked about my upbringing and about my parents. I knew he was gauging the man I was. As Mrs. Harvey mentioned, I was the first man Leslyn had ever brought home. I was sure Mr. Harvey was trying to see what made me special to her.

"So, what's going on with you and Johanna?"

With a chuckle, I replied, "I don't even know anymore. And it's my fault."

Adjusting in his seat, he stared at me pensively. "How so?"

I explained the fake relationship with Lyric and how Leslyn found out. It was probably foolish to tell the father of the woman I loved that I did some fuck boy shit. But I trusted Mr. Harvey to tell me the truth.

For a moment, he sat in silence, staring at the starry sky above. He continued to smoke his cigar and sip his whisky, so I did the same.

"It's not your fault," he said, breaking the silence.

"Nah, it is. I knew she had trust issues and I still did what I did."

He shook his head fervently. "No. I'm saying it's my fault she has trust issues." My eyebrows met as I tried to piece everything together. "The reason we moved here was because Jennifer thought it would save our marriage. She believed a new state, new house, and new jobs would help our struggling marriage. We were having trouble conceiving and it put a strain on us. Leslyn was not happy about the move, and truthfully, she had every right to be upset. Jennifer uprooted her life to run from our problems. The problems followed and six months after the move, we were back to not speaking."

Mr. Harvey expelled a long, deep sigh before bringing his glass to his lips.

"I had this colleague, Debra. She was charismatic, beautiful, and smart. We worked closely together, and it wasn't long before our conversations become more about our personal lives and less about work. At this point, Jennifer and I weren't sleeping together, and every conversation turned into an argument. Leslyn was watching her parents grow apart, and her reaction was to spend less time at home. She joined every club and became a cheerleader. There were days when we wouldn't even see each other. The entire household was disconnected. I started working later, and so did Debra."

I shook my head, afraid of where this story was going. Leslyn told me about this rough patch with her parents, but she never went into great detail about it. Now, I saw why she glossed over that part of her life. Watching your family fall apart was never easy. For years, I watched it happen with my parents.

"One evening, Jennifer and Johanna wanted to surprise me with dinner in the city. I was working late with Debra. Jennifer and I had an argument that morning, and I was still fuming. Debra was extra flirty that day. Her laughs were lighter, touches were more sensual, and skirt was a little tighter. We were having a casual conversation that went left and I let it. She took a seat on the corner of my desk and pulled me between her legs. I knew I fucked up. There wasn't time for me to say no and come back to my right mind before my baby girl caught us."

The hurt in his eyes as he explained Leslyn's reaction.

"It took years of me begging for forgiveness and family therapy before we got over it. I had to fight for my family. My wife didn't trust me, and my baby girl couldn't bear to look at me. It was really a dark time for us all."

"Damn," was all I could say.

We went back to silence as I mulled over everything he'd shared.

"Johanna is a tough young woman. It's because we raised her that way. She knows what she wants, and how to get it."

I nodded, agreeing with everything he said about Leslyn.

"I've done my best to show her I'm serious about us. Leslyn is different, and she knows it. But I don't know to prove to her I'm different, and that I won't hurt her."

"She knows it. Your being here with us proves that. Just give her more time. She'll come around."

Mr. Harvey refilled our glasses and we continued smoking our cigars. Luckily, the topic changed, and so did my mood.

His words rang in my ears about giving Leslyn more time, and I hoped he was right.

7

"What are you so afraid of, Johanna?"

My eyebrows furrowed and I backed away from my mother's vanity. We were in her bathroom going through her perfume. After her putting me on the spot, we came upstairs to talk. I apologized for raising my voice and she apologized for being pushy.

I knew my parents loved Ogun. He was smart, had a magnetic personality, and respectful. There was never a time that he came over without a gift for them. He was also the only man I'd ever introduced to them. They met him at my graduation celebration so I knew they wouldn't think too much of our friendship, but once the trips became more frequent, my mother became more curious.

I invited him to dinner to prove to my parents and to myself that we were just friends. Seeing him with my parents only deepened my feelings for him. It also confirmed my mother's suspicions about us.

"Ma, what are you talking about?" I sat on the chaise in her walk-in closet.

"Ogun. What are you afraid of?"

My nostrils flared as I took in a deep breath. She knew what I was afraid of happening. My parents and I were doing great. Their marital issues scarred me, probably more than they ever realized.

The love they shared was the purest, deepest love I'd ever known. That was until they'd changed. The happy, loving home that I knew had changed in an instant. They couldn't talk without arguing, were sleeping in separate rooms, and I became an afterthought. But the thing that hurt me most was seeing my father with his coworker. Our family was falling apart, and he was falling into the arms of another woman.

It took years for me to forgive him. Meanwhile, my mother forgave him almost instantly. I knew there were conversations that happened behind my back, but the optics weren't pretty. While they moved on and repaired their marriage, I was still left with questions. My parents raised me to have standards, and to let no one treat me less than, yet my father broke a vow and my mother just… forgave him.

"I'm afraid of getting my heartbroken. It's terrifying to think that one day, I might not be enough for him. I'm not like you, Ma. I wouldn't be able to just forgive him and act like it never happened."

My mother's eyebrows met as she walked over to me. Cupping my cheek, she said, "Oh, honey. That's not what happened at all."

"Well, that's what it looked it. And once I left for college, you two were back like Daddy never cheated."

"It took far longer for us to bounce back than you think."

"Why did you stay? You always told me not to put up with any disrespect."

"It's... complicated, baby."

With a sigh, I replied, "I'm not a child anymore, and this situation is part of the reason I'm so scared to commit. Until this point, I could keep men at a distance. I got what I needed from them and moved on to the next. But Ogun, he's different. Somehow, he's been able to break through the wall I've built to protect my heart. I've fallen for him, and that is terrifying because I'm not sure how it would end."

"I was able to forgive him because we both were in an awful place then. I put all my time and energy into making this house a home and focusing on getting my degree that I neglected him and you. We allowed our frustrations with not being able to conceive push us apart, when we should've been closer than ever. Relationships are complicated, baby. I had to decide if I wanted to continue the life I created with your father or move on. For me, I was willing to fight for my marriage, and your father did too. We messed up by not being considerate of how you were handling everything. Honestly, after family therapy, I thought you were fine. Now, I see that isn't the case."

She reached for my hands, pulling me up from the chaise. I laid my head on her shoulder as she hugged me.

"Des thinks Aubrey is cheating on her," I said after a moment.

While I considered all the girls to be my best friends, Destinee held a special place in my heart. She was my roommate freshman year, and we got our first apartment together. When she broke the news that they were moving, I was less than thrilled, but I understood. I was never too fond of Aubrey, but as long as my girl was happy, so was I. Only now she wasn't happy. And she was alone in a new state with no one to comfort her.

I wished I could've been there for her.

I wished there was more I could do other than offer a listening ear.

"You have to let Destinee figure that out on her own. I know it's your nature to protect the ones you loved, but unless she's ready to leave, there isn't anything you can say or do to change her mind." My mother cupped my cheeks, her slanted maple eyes boring into mine. "Now, go downstairs and tell that man how you feel."

"I want to, but what if—"

"No 'what if's', baby. I have a feeling that he will understand where you're coming from."

In my twenty-three years of living, rarely was my mother wrong. Instead of questioning her, I took her advice and we headed downstairs to join the guys on the porch. My father poured us whisky and we sat outside and talked until midnight.

By the time we made it back to my apartment, I was dreading saying goodbye to Ogun. His flight was in a few hours and we hadn't talked about the next time we'd see each other.

While Ogun made himself comfortable on my couch, I went to my room and changed. When I returned, he was typing a text, visibly irritated by whatever he was handling. I sat on the arm of the couch and waited for him to finish.

"I'm doing the video," he said, falling back onto the couch, and sighing. "David and Amani were able to convince Lyric to change a few scenes, including me having a solo."

"When are y'all shooting it?"

"In three days." Brushing his hand over his face, he looked at me with pensive eyes. Reaching for my hand, he pulled me onto his lap and wrapped his arms around my waist. "I'm glad I came this weekend."

"Me too," I whispered. Warmth covered my body from the kisses he trailed down my neck. "We needed this time together."

Ogun pulled back and I adjusted myself on his lap so I could see him. I ran the back of my hand along his beard while smiling. My heart jolted when his full lips curved into a half-smile. His grip on my waist tightened, causing my breath to hitch.

I loved him.

Damn.

"What are we doing, Les?" Breaking eye contact, I sighed. "I'm not trying to fall back into this same cycle."

"Cycle?"

"Yeah, we come so close to finally admitting what it is between us, then one of us retreats. Last time it was me, this time it's you."

"You know how I feel about you, Ogun."

"Tell me," he said throatily.

Swallowing the lump in my throat, I told him, "I'm in love with you and have been for a while now, but I'm scared for either of us to get hurt. This shit is so new to me–"

Ogun's lips crashed into mine. His kisses were slow and intoxicating. Every reason I had for why we shouldn't be together slipped my mind. There were no thoughts clouding my mind. I just lived in the moment. I let the feeling of his warm lips and soft caresses guide me to the right decision. I wanted him and he wanted me. Yes, relationships got complicated sometimes, but the truth of the matter was that we were meant to be together.

"I love you, too," he confessed, brushing his lips against mine.

An instant smile spread across my mouth. Ogun

gently held my chin and kissed me once more. This time, our kiss was more heated. As our tongues slowly danced together, his hands slipped under my t-shirt. With Ogun's help, I repositioned myself on his lap. Now facing him, we stared at each other.

"I'm all about you, and you're enough for me. No one else matters. Not Lyric, not your parents, nobody. You get me?"

My cheeks warmed and goosebumps covered my skin as I nodded. Ogun's left hand rested on the small of my back while the right wrapped around my neck.

"You ain't gotta be afraid of hurting me or anything like that, and vice versa. This shit is solid."

My response was to kiss him hard and messily. He met my fire, literally kissing my breath away as I melted into him. A smile covered his lips when I rocked against his hardened dick. Ogun pulled my shirt over my head before removing his own.

In one swift motion, I was on my back, the rest of our clothes were on the floor, and he was inside of me. My eyes rolled to the back of my head as I prepared myself for the inevitable pleasure Ogun would bring me.

———

"So, what happens now?" I asked, running slow circles along his stomach.

Ogun sighed. "We keep doin' what we're doin'. There's nothing that needs to change between us. I'll continue to fly you out whenever you want, call you every day, and continue to make time for you."

"Nothing will change," I repeated to myself.

Ogun hummed and pulled me on top of him. The slither of light coming through my blinds gave me just enough light to see his features. His eyes were low, and eyebrows drew together. There was something on his mind. Hopefully not something that would ruin the moment.

"Your father told me what happened."

A sigh fell from my lips as I laid on his chest. "I don't want to talk about it," I told him.

"But I do."

"What is there to talk about? I've forgiven him and we have moved on."

"Nah," Ogun said flatly. "You haven't moved on and I don't want it to come up when we have problems or a disagreement. We've talked about my trust issues and why I have them. Now, it's your turn."

"I was so hurt because I figured that if my father couldn't be faithful, no man could. Everything he ever told me about love and relationships was bullshit after that. Even after he and my mother worked it out, I held on to what happened. I don't know why it took so long for me to let it go. And yes, I see how holding on to that hurt has messed me up. It made me bitter, and I put every man in that box because of it. I almost missed out on the best thing that's ever happened to me."

I raised my head to meet his gaze.

"It was never supposed to get this deep, but it did

and that scared me. Then, I saw you with Lyric, and the only person I could blame was myself. In your own way, you've showed me what I meant to you. I mean, you wrote a whole song about me," I said with a laugh out of pure frustration because all the signs were there.

Ogun hummed and wrapped his arms around me. "Like I said before, the past is the past. We were both playing games."

"No more games," I said against his lips.

He kissed me, then said, "No more."

*M*y heart thumped against my chest and my eyes widened as my lips curved into a smile. Kassandra shrieked as we looked over our appearances in the mirror. We'd spent hours in hair and makeup getting ready for Ogun's album release party. Tonight was the first night Ogun and I would be out as a couple. No longer was I the mystery woman in the blogs. I was still figuring out how I felt about it. Beyond the obvious feeling of nervousness, I felt anxious about walking through the crowd on Ogun's arm.

"Les, you look bomb as fuck!" Kassandra said, nodding.

My cheeks warmed as I fluffed my curls. I knew Ogun wanted to go all out tonight, but I didn't expect him to give me the royal treatment. Since I'd landed last night, I'd gotten a massage, a manicure, and pedicure; and I'd been in hair and makeup all afternoon. The icing on the cake was the off-the-shoulder navy dress Ogun's assistant dropped off for me.

Kassandra was right.

I looked like a bag of money.

"Thanks, friend. You do, too."

She smiled and smoothed her hand down her black silk dress.

"Amani out did himself with this dress," she noted while doing a quick spin in the mirror.

After snapping a few pictures, we left our room and went down the hall to meet the boys. Ogun's schedule had been crazy the last few weeks. He still made time for us to have a weekend together, but I understood how busy it got around album release time. When Kassandra and I entered their suite, Ogun was on the balcony doing an interview. His gaze met mine and he smiled. I waved while blushing before joining Kassandra at the bar and waited for him to wrap up.

Yesterday, he recorded 'A Day in the Life of Ogun' where Vogue followed him around for the day. He spent the day doing press, photoshoots, and having meetings with his team. Even after all that, he was on time to pick me up from the airport.

"He's eager for everyone to hear his album tonight," Amani said to me.

When it came to his music, he was super protective of it. Even I had heard none of it aside from the song he'd recorded for me. Ogun took his art seriously, and I respected it.

"I know. Every time he talks about it, he lights up. He deserves all the love he's getting."

"Yeah, he does. Especially after the last album."

I nodded, taking a glass of wine that Kassandra had poured for me. Ogun deserved to bask in this moment. He'd been through a lot over the past year. I was just happy to be by his side through it all. We were there for each other at our lowest points, and now we were reaping the benefits of our success together.

Once he finished his interview, he joined us for a drink before he had to finish getting dressed. We spoke briefly until his stylist called him to the room. Amani, Kassandra, and I continued to talk while we waited. The suite was packed with people from Ogun's stylists, assistants, and members of his family. It was a lot to take in. I wasn't sure if I would be able to keep calm with all that going on around me, but he handled it with ease.

I was laughing at a joke Amani made when Ogun poked his head from the room and called out for me. I placed my glass down, then made my way over to him. The bedroom was filled with racks of clothes and boxes of shoes. Ogun's assistant and stylist were going back and forth over an outfit. I looked to Ogun and he just shook his head.

"Which shirt do you like?" he asked, exasperated.

He held up two navy shirts.

The first one was a plain silk shirt, and the second had an intricate design with various shades of blue. I looked next at the pants that were laid out on the bed. The first pair were a cream color made of linen, and the other pants were black.

"The second shirt with the cream pants," I told him.

Next, I went to the desk where his jewelry was spread out. "These chains," I pointed at the silver Cuban links. "And this watch." I held up the iced-out Rolex.

Ogun smiled and told everyone to clear the room.

"They were lowkey pissin' me off. I told them to have this shit ready a week ago." Brushing his hand over his face, he walked over to me. "You good? Need anything? I know it's been a lot going on since you landed."

"I'm fine. Are you good? You're the main attraction tonight."

He answered by kissing me sweetly and deeply. I had to end our kiss so he could get dressed. While he put on his shirt and pants, I gathered his jewelry for him. After putting on his chains and watch, he went in the closet and came out with a box.

"What's this?" I asked, taking it from him.

"Open it."

He grinned and ran his hand over his locs that were styled into four cornrows.

I untied the red bow, then opened the top. My jaw dropped at the smaller green box inside.

"You know I had to get you one, Ifemi," he said as he came over to me.

Ogun opened the Rolex box. Butterflies swarmed my belly, and a smile spread across my face. The silver watch had a light pink face and was gorgeous. Gently, he slid the watch on my wrist and closed the clasp. Holding up my wrist, I beamed from ear to ear. Ogun hugged me from behind and kissed my cheek.

After he finished getting dressed, everyone took pictures, then we headed to the club for the listening party. During the ride, Amani warned me and Kassandra about the chaos that was waiting outside the club. Even after his warning, the amount of paparazzi and screaming fans still surprised me. Ogun held my waist while we posed for a few pictures before ushering me inside.

"This is a lot," I said through my smile.

His grip on my waist remained firm. "It's okay, baby. I got you."

As soon as we made it inside, Ogun's manager David whisked him away, and Amani led me to the booth where Kassandra was seated. Kassandra wrapped her arm around me and handed me a flute of champagne. I was thankful for the drink because shortly after, Ogun reintroduced me to his parents as his girlfriend. His mother hugged me, while his father just offered a nod. I could see in his father's eyes he was proud of Ogun for finally settling down.

Most of the night, I stayed with Kassandra while Ogun worked the room. It felt good partying with my girl Kassandra with my man close by. Ogun posed for pictures and did a few interviews before going on stage to speak. We had a booth next to the stage where Ogun stood thanking everyone. I watched him in awe.

On stage was the man I met a year ago in Miami. Adorned in dark shades, a grill, and confidence that I loved so much. He spent a few moments talking about what the album meant to him and shared a few videos of him in the studio. His team put together a video documenting the entire recording process. I was proud of him for showing his process. He ended the speech by calling me to the stage. I looked at Kassandra who smiled, then nudged for me to go on stage.

Reaching for my hand, Ogun pulled me into his side.

"Last, I want to thank Leslyn, Ifemi, my love, publicly for holding me down throughout this process. We all know I'm one of those moody artists who gets sucked into the process." Everyone laughed. "She helped me find my muse, supported me when I was distant, and is a constant reminder of why I need to slow down and enjoy life. I love you, Leslyn, and I wouldn't have made it this far without you by my side."

He kissed me and the crowd erupted into cheers and applause.

"I can't believe you just put me on the spot like that," I said in his ear.

Ogun smiled. "You know I had to show my baby some love."

Warmth spread in my cheeks and a smile formed on my lips.

With his arm thrown over my shoulder, we walked back to our booth.

Before getting pulled away by his manager, Ogun told me, "This is only the beginning, Ifemi."

My stomach fluttered.

I could only imagine what was in store for us.

THE END

Thank you for taking the time to read Take You Down!

If you enjoyed this story, I ask that you consider leaving a review on Amazon and/or Goodreads.

Until next time,

D.

ACKNOWLEDGMENTS

God, for this gift!

Bria,#DRIA4L. LY.

Shanice, for always being in my corner rooting for me.

TWC, the greatest accountability partners a writer could ask for!

Eddie, for supporting me through my long days and nights of writing, revising, & editing!

Family and friends, for you alls unwavering support <3

STAY CONNECTED

Text **Rosebud** to 33777 to subscribe to my mailing list.

www.authordrose.com

Follow me on social media:

facebook.com/AuthorDRose
twitter.com/authordrose
instagram.com/whoisdrose

Share My World

Pieces of Love

Love on Repeat

Made in the USA
Columbia, SC
15 May 2025

57942422R00071